FAMOUS

A PAULA WISEMAN BOOK
New York · London · Toronto · Sydney · New Delhi

Daddycated to Rebecca and Jessica

SIMON & SCHUSTER BOOKS FOR YOUNG READERS
An imprint of Simon & Schuster Children's Publishing Division
1230 Avenue of the Americas, New York, New York 10020
Copyright © 2015 by Ronald Barrett
SIMON & SCHUSTER BOOKS FOR YOUNG READERS is a trademark of Simon & Schuster, Inc.
For information about special discounts for bulk purchases, please contact
Simon & Schuster Special Sales at 1-866-506-1949 or business@simonandschuster.com.
The Simon & Schuster Speakers Bureau can bring authors to your live event. For more information
or to book an event, contact the Simon & Schuster Speakers Bureau at
1-866-248-3049 or visit our website at www.simonspeakers.com.
Book design by Lucy Ruth Cummins
The text for this book is set in Gill Sans Std.
The illustrations for this book are rendered in pencil, watercolor, and ink.
Manufactured in China
0615 SCP
2 4 6 8 10 9 7 5 3 1
Library of Congress Cataloging-in-Publication Data
Barrett, Ron, author, illustrator.
Cats get famous / Ron Barrett.—1st edition.
pages cm
"A Paula Wiseman Book." 9231
Summary: Disguised as a trash bag, greedy cat-hater Lekvar Smirk kidnaps a trio of singing cats,
Hal, Dora, and Geneva, and takes them to try out for the television show *Animal Idol*.
ISBN 978-1-4424-9453-4 (hardcover)
ISBN 978-1-4424-9454-1 (eBook)
[1. Cats—Fiction. 2. Singers—Fiction. 3. Fame—Fiction. 4. Kidnapping—Fiction.
5. Greed—Fiction. 6. Humorous stories.] 1. Title.
PZ7.B275346Cam 2015
[E]—dc23
2014022764

nce upon a fence there was a trio of cats: Hal, Dora, and Geneva. They never wanted to do anything else but sing together, because that made them happier than anything else.

They felt loved by everyone. But their singing was not loved by everyone because it kept people awake at night.

One of those people was Lekvar Smirk. He hated the cats'
singing, but he liked animals who could do unusual things—he put them into
concerts and circuses and took them to TV talent contests.
He also liked keeping a large part of the money they earned.

Lekvar Smirk thought they would be perfect for the TV show *Animal Idol*.

He disguised himself as a trash bag . . .

and captured the clueless Hal, Dora, and Geneva.

He took them to a theater where
the tryouts were held.

**When they arrived, there were other animals
waiting to perform for the judges.**

Lekvar greedily eyed the cash prize the cats could win,
and thought of the huge share he would take.

When it was the cats' turn,
Lekvar pushed them into
the spotlight and said,
"Sing good and loud."

The cats sang more loud than good.
The judges weren't thrilled, but they needed to fill a space on the show.

The other chosen animals were Yolanda and Don,
two horses who danced on roller skates;

Bernice, an acrobatic ant; and Rabs, a saxophone-playing rabbit.

Lekvar decided that the only way the cats would win was if he made the other contestants lose.

He loosened the wheels on Yolanda's and Don's skates.

He put butter on Bernice's trapeze . . .

and water into Rabs's saxophone.

When the show began, everything went wrong for the contestants.

So when Hal, Dora, and Geneva sang and didn't fall on a judge

or spray anyone, they were voted the winners.

The cats were happy to be **Animal Idols** and left the theater.
Lekvar called after them, "Wait a minute, cats, I can get you a concert at
the Ridiculously Grand Hotel in Las Vegas."

But the cats had
other ideas.

Dora, who loved fashion, used her cash prize
to open a boutique, Fence-y Fashions.

Hal, who loved food,
opened a restaurant,
Hal's Dumpster Diner.

And Geneva, who loved being loved, opened hearts by acting in films.

But fame had its misfortune. The cats longed for their happy days making music together in the alleyway.

**One day, Hal was passing a garbage can
and spotted a tasty-looking piece of birthday cake.**

Under the cake was Dora. There was Geneva, too.

The trio was together again.
"We were great," Hal said.
"We were Animal Idols, top of the heap," said Dora.

"Yeah, but it was even greater
when we made music together in
the alleyway," said Geneva.
And they all agreed.

Hal, Dora, and Geneva decided to close their businesses, give up acting, and go back to the alleyway.

**Only now they added a new kind of song
to their repertoire—the lullaby . . .**

which pleased their audience enormously.

Lekvar might even have heard it in his jail cell.

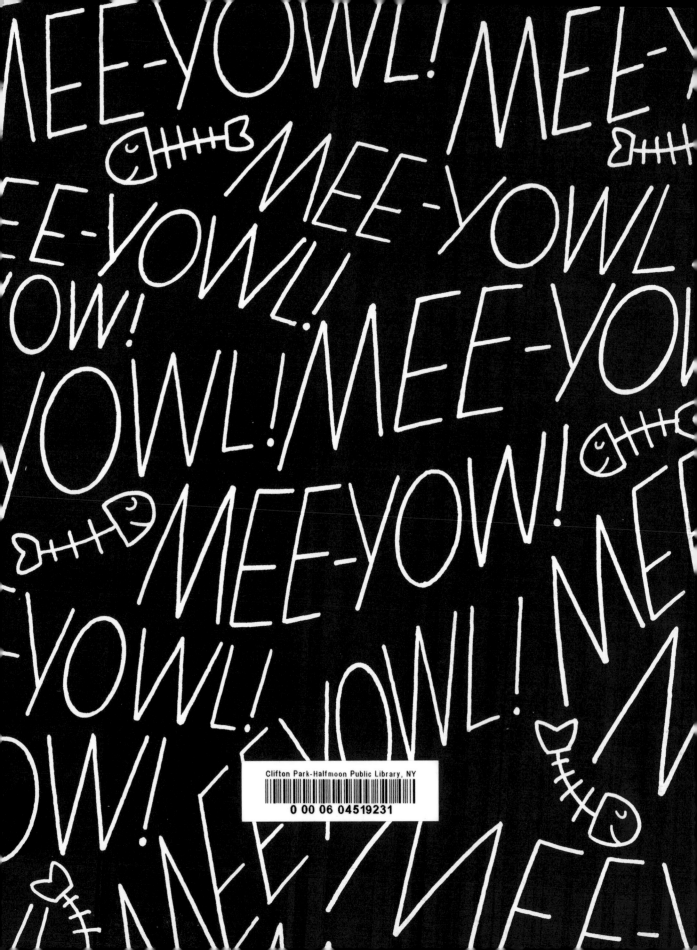